ELLA

Diaries

TOP SECRET!

Meredith Costain

For Mo Johnson—and my family,
for many wonderful Christmases!—M.C.

For Ray, Jade and Zoe x—D.M.

Danielle McDonald

Scholastic Australia
345 Pacific Highway Lindfield NSW 2070
An imprint of Scholastic Australia Pty Limited
PO Box 579 Gosford NSW 2250
ABN 11 000 614 577
www.scholastic.com.au

Part of the Scholastic Group
Sydney · Auckland · New York · Toronto · London · Mexico City
· New Delhi · Hong Kong · Buenos Aires · Puerto Rico

Published by Scholastic Australia in 2016.
Text copyright © Meredith Costain, 2016.
Illustrations copyright © Danielle McDonald, 2016.

National Library of Australia Cataloguing-in-Publication entry

Creator: Costain, Meredith, 1955- author.
Title: Operation Merry Christmas / Meredith Costain; illustrated by Danielle McDonald.
ISBN: 9781760159580 (paperback)
Series: Costain, Meredith, 1955- Ella diaries; 9.
Target Audience: For primary school age.
Subjects: Christmas stories.
Vacations--Juvenile fiction.
Other Creators/Contributors: McDonald, Danielle, illustrator.
Dewey Number: A823.3

Typeset in Sweetie Pie.

Printed by McPherson's Printing Group, Maryborough, VIC.

Scholastic Australia's policy, in association with McPherson's Printing Group, is to use papers that are renewable and made efficiently from wood grown in responsibly managed forests, so as to minimise its environmental footprint.

10 9 8 7 6 5 4   16 17 18 19 20 / 1

MIX
Paper from
responsible sources
FSC
www.fsc.org   FSC® C001695

ELLA

Diaries

OPERATION
Merry Christmas

Friday night, in bed, just before lights out

Dear Diary,

It's nearly Christmas. I love Christmas!

THINGS I LOVE ABOUT CHRISTMAS

 Presents.  ←--- **presents**

 Christmas decorations EVERYWHERE. Especially sparkly ones.

3 People walking around with happy, smiling faces, humming Christmas tunes.

Every year we stay in this sweet little caravan park in Moonlight Bay for the Christmas holidays.

I go rock-pooling

Rock pool

and whizz around on the rides at the carnival

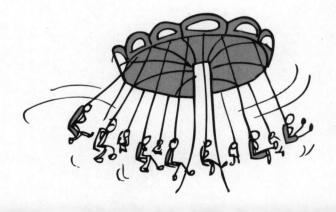

and eat yummy food at the
Christmas market

Yummy

and sing carols on the beach.

But guess what?

Da da da . . . dummmm.

This morning Mum got some horrifically
horrifying BAD NEWS.

✻ 6 ✻

The Bad News

Moonlight Gardens Caravan Park is closing down.

The Badderer News

We will be staying home for Christmas this year instead. That means

NO beach.

NO carnival rides.

NO yummy market food.

NOOOOOOOoo.........

Everyone in my family is SHOCKED.

Especially Mum.

Shock Meter

(The shockedest)

MUM

Dad

ME

Olivia

Max

BOB

That's because Mum has been going to Moonlight Bay for Christmas every year since she was a little girl (about 900 years ago). Mum LOVES Moonlight Bay, even more than I do.

It is BREAKING her HEART, Diary! I saw her having a sad little cry about it while she was chopping up onions for our dinner tonight. (Onions. Bleuchhh.)

So tonight I made a special secret promise to myself.

I, Ella, do solemnly promise that I will do everything in my power to make sure that THIS YEAR (even though we are stuck at home in our boring house in our boring street with no beach or rock pools or sandy places where you can bury your annoying brother and/or sister up to their necks if they do annoying stuff like follow you around everywhere) we will ALL have the BEST CHRISTMAS EVER!!!

Signed: Ella

There are only **18 days** till Christmas.
So I will start tomorrow.
(Cross my heart hope to die.)

Good night, Diary.
Sweet dreams.
Love,
Ella xxx

Friday night, a bit later

Dearest Diary,

I can't stop thinking about my special secret promise.

So I have come up with an amazing, fantabulously fabulous scheme✳ to make Christmas betterer. I have decided to call it
Operation Merry Christmas!
(OMC for short.)

✳ So far I've only worked out the first part.

OMC STAGE ONE :

Decorate the HOUSE with ★ Beautiful Decorations

Then Mum will be SO DAZZLED by all the sparkly, glittery stuff she will forget about poor SOLD Moonlight Gardens Caravan Park.

This will be easy-peasy because we already have lots of ~~extreemly~~ extremely attractive Christmas decorations. They live in a big box at the very top of the toppest cupboard in the hallway.

what could possibly go wrong?

E

Saturday morning, before breakfast

Dear Diary,

I woke up really, really early so I could start
OMC STAGE ONE.

The first thing I did was put on my special
slippers with the super-sneaky silent soles.
Then I silently sneaked
down the hallway so I
could get the Christmas
decorations out of the
cupboard before Mum
and Dad woke up.

SPECIAL
SLIPPERS

super-
sneaky
SILENT SOLES

~~unforch~~ Unfortunately, it was WAY too tall for me to reach.

BOX of

Christmas **DECORATIONS**

(inside **CUPBOARD** at the **very** top)

TOPPEST CUPBOARD

ME

So I went into ninja stealth mode and crept (super stealthily) into the kitchen and brought back a dining chair to stand on.

Dining Chair

But I still wasn't tall enough. So I crept back to the kitchen (even more super stealthily) and grabbed a stool and put it on top of the chair.

Kitchen STOOL

Dining CHAIR

I STILL wasn't tall enough. So I climbed down again and crept into the lounge room and got some nice big, thick books from the bookcase. Then I put the books on top of the stool.

BiG THICK BOOKS

And then I climbed up onto the top of the books and stood on the very tippiest part of my tippy-toes.

I was just reaching up to open the cupboard door when somebody screamed behind me. Like this:

So I screamed back. Like this:

Only LOUDER, because they gave me a
fright.

And then the somebody (who was ~~acksh~~
actually my dad) said,

And I said, 'Trying to get something out of the cupboard.'

And Dad said, 'I thought you were a ~~bugler~~ burglar! Get down now before you fall off and hurt yourself!'

And I said, 'It's OK, I'm extra good at balancing on top of very tall things.' *

* which is actually 100% true, because of all the leaps and flips and jumps I do every week on top of the balance beam at Twisters.

Then I reached up even higherer and opened the cupboard door.

Reaching even HIGHER...

~~unforch~~ Unfortunately, when the door opened the box tipped over and everything inside it fell out.

All over Dad.

Dad the GIGANTEROUS christmas TREE ★

Oops.

Hehe. He looked just like a giganterous Christmas tree. ☺☺☺

Saturday morning, after breakfast

Dear Diary,

I am in **BiG TROUBLE**.

THINGS I AM IN BIG TROUBLE FOR

① Doing riskerous things, like climbing up dangerous furniture to reach tall cupboards. (Even though I am one of the best balancers in the history of balancing.)

2 Creeping around the house like a burglar when I am supposed to be asleep in bed.

BURGLAR (ME)!

3 Scaring Dad. (And also laughing at him. Which is really unfair because he DID look EXACTLY like a Christmas tree. And Olivia and Max laughed when they saw him too. How come THEY'RE not in BIG TROUBLE??)

BOB

After I'd finished un-decorating Dad, Mum put the box of Christmas decorations away. Only more carefully this time.

And then she said if I was very, VERY good and unriskerous for the rest of the week, I could do the decorating NEXT weekend. MAybe.

WAAAAAAHHH!

It's SO not fair, Diary. There are only **17 days** days to go until Christmas. I want to get started RIGHT NOW!

How am I supposed to make **OMC** STAGE ONE work if I can't put up the glitterised tinsel or the sweet little Christmas ~~borbels~~ baubles or the ho-ho-ho-ing Santas?

I need to have an Emergency Meeting with Zoe (my BFF) ~~as soon as possible~~ immediately. Zoe ALWAYS has exceptionally excellent ideas about importerant stuff like this.

Talk later, Diary.
Ella

Saturday night, in bed

Dear Diary,

I rang Zoe and asked her to come over IMMEDIATELY as I was in desperating despair (as well as BIG TROUBLE). Preferably with emergency snacks.

After we'd eaten the snacks, I explained about OMC and how it was looking hopelessly hopeless because all our Christmas decorations were locked away for another WHOLE WEEK inside a tall, dark cupboard.

Zoe's forehead part went all crinkly and
serious which meant her brain was doing
DEEP THINKING.

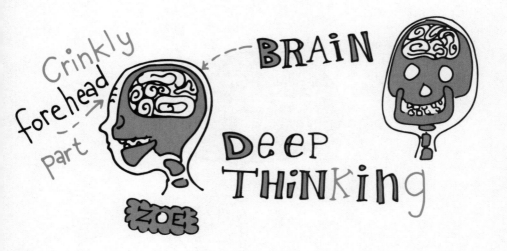

Crinkly
forehead
part

BRAIN

DEEP
THINKING

ZOE

Then she looked at
me with shiny eyes
(like the glittery bits
in those Christmas
baubles that look just

shiny
eyes

like the mirror balls they have at the Year 6 Graduation Dance, only smaller) and said, 'I know! We can make our OWN Christmas decorations! Right now!'

And I said,

ZOE, you are BRILLIANT!

And Zoe said, 'I KNOW!'

So we did!

Here is a picture of the sweet little reindeer we made using old toilet rolls, and twigs we found out in the garden. They look aMAZing.

Twigs

Googly EYES

Toilet roll

Dasher

* Glitter

Pom Pom!

Smasher

Crasher

Then we painted our fingernails with assorted nail polishes to look like Christmas decorations!

CHRISTMAS
Nail Polish
DESIGNS ⭐

ZOE'S
Favourite

My
favourite

And we made homemade tinsel out of popcorn and bits of string!

POPCORN String

Tinsel

The Bad News

Bob kept trying to play fetch with the reindeer twigs.

The Bad News

BOB

DAD'S FEET

REINDEER

The Badder News

And he ate most of the popcorn tinsel when no-one was looking.

The Badderer News

I accidentally left my box of assorted nail polishes in a place

where Max could find them. And Max found them. And then he used them to draw a duck* on the lounge-room wall.

* Or maybe it was a rabbit. Or a duck-rabbit.

And then I made a BIG mess trying to clean it off with nail-polish removerer before Mum saw it.

And then I made an even BIGGER mess trying to clean the first mess up with a giganterous bottle of STAIN removerer I found in the bathroom cupboard.

STAIN
REMOVERER

STAINO

Some of the stain removerer accidentally spilt on the carpet. So now the carpet is a bit patcherous and spotty and looks like a leopard. ☹

The ~~Worserer~~ Worse News

Mum saw it. And now I am in even BIGGER trouble.

☹☹☹☹☹

Saturday night, about half an hour later

Dear Diary,

I can't sleep. There are too many thoughts whizzing around my brain.

INSIDE
MY
BRAIN

So far, **Operation Merry Christmas** is going really, really badly. Instead of cheering up Mum, I've just made her cross. ☹

Good night, Diary.

E

Sunday, before lunch

Dad and I spent all morning trying to turn the leopard carpet in the lounge room back into just a carpet again.

Sunday, after lunch

Guess what? Zoe just rang me to say she's had ANOTHER brilliant idea for OMC! And she's coming over in ten minutes so we can have another Emergency Meeting to start planning STAGE TWO.

ANOTHER BRILLIANT IDEA

I can't wait!!!

Sunday, about five minutes later

Mum says that as I am officially in BIG(GER) TROUBLE, Zoe is only allowed to come over on two (2) STRICT CONDITIONS.

STRICT CONDITION NUMBER

We are not allowed to use, or even THINK about using, any craft materials (including ANY of the following) without her or Dad's STRICT SUPERVISION:

Scissors

marker pens

COLOURED PENCILS

POPCORN

TOILET ROLLS

Googly EYES

Glitter

sticky TAPE

TWIGS

POM POMS

ASSORTED NAIL POLISH

← * ESPECIALLY THIS ONE!

STRICT CONDITION NUMBER

We have to stay away from tall cupboards and/or not do anything RISKEROUS.

I have to go now and get ready before Zoe gets here!

Talk soon!
Ella

Sunday night

Dear Diary,

Just when I thought we had the perfect plan for STAGE TWO of OMC, everything went wrong. Again. ☹

Here's what happened at our Emergency Meeting:

Zoe: I have another BRILLIANT idea for OMC. Guess what it is!
Me: We are going to set up Santa's Workshop right here in our house and invite all his elves to make us presents?

Zoe: Nope. Guess again.

Me: We are going to cover our whole house with twinkly lights that flash on and off? And put a giganterous sleigh on top of the roof? With a giganterous Santa climbing down the chimney?

Giganterous SLEIGH

Santa

Zoe: Nope. Guess again.

Me: We are going to get all of Mum's favourite bands—bleuchhh—to sing Christmas carols in front of our house?

Zoe: Nope. Not even close.

Me (not quite so exciterated): I give up. What???

Zoe: It's easy-peasy!
SNOW!!!
Me: Snow???

And then Zoe explained
how she and her family
watched a funny Christmas movie last
night. Only the people in the movie lived
in a place where it was cold and wintry
at Christmas-time, instead of warm and
summery like it is here. So they were
always doing excellent
and funnerous things like
having snowball fights and
building sweet little snow
people with carrots for noses.

So Zoe said that if we could have snow at OUR HOUSE at Christmas, it would be really different and UN-boring and special! SO special Mum would want to frolic around in it and have snowball fights with her kind and thoughtful daughter (me).

And because it would be even more exciterating than the sand and rock pools and beach at Moonlight Bay, no-one would be sad or gloomerous that we stayed home this year.

And I said,

And Zoe smiled
modestly* and
said, 'I know.'

MODEST
Smile

* 'Modest' means not telling everyone else
how fantabulously fabulous and marvellous
and excellent you are all the time, like one
ANNOYING girl in my
class does, especially
when she is sucking up
to the teachers (which is
~~most~~ all of the time).

Peach Parker

And then we started talking about all the
aMAZing and fanTABulously FABulous fun
things we could do in the snow, like:

① Making beautiful snow angels.

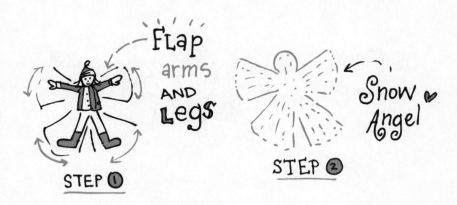

FLAP arms AND Legs

STEP ①

Snow Angel

STEP ②

② Going tobogganing using the top of the rubbish bin as a toboggan.

US

WHEEEEEE

RUBBISH BIN LID!

Tobogganing

3 Building a giganterous snow fort with buckets and spades, and hiding inside it!

US hiding

Spade

Bucket

SNOW FORT

And then I had a seriously serious thought:

Where were we going to get ALL THAT snow FROM?

I told Zoe my serious thought. And guess what she said?

And then she told me all about this science program called *Wacky Science* she watches on TV, where they show you how to make scientifical things like rotten-egg gas (eww) and exploding volcanoes in jars. And this week they made snow. And Zoe said it was EASY-PEASY.

All you needed was two super-special secret ingredients:

PAPER
TOWELS

WATER

This is what we said next:

Me (confused): Snow? Out of paper towels? How would they even be cold enough?
Zoe: I don't know. The TV show didn't explain that bit. They just said to tear off ten sheets of paper towel and make them all wet and then put them in a food blenderiser.

Me (looking at Zoe like she had just had part of her brain removed and replaced with a jam donut): You never said anything about a food blenderiser. And anyway, we don't even have a food blenderiser. Mum just mashes things up with a fork.

Zoe: Maybe we could just tear the bits of paper towel up into teeny tiny pieces with our fingers instead?

Me: Good idea.

So we got some paper towel from the kitchen and tore it up into little bits.

Then we poured cold water over them.

Now we have a small pile of teeny tiny pieces of soggy paper towel that looks like this.

But no snow. ☹

Soggy paper towel

Monday afternoon, after school

Dearest Diary,

Two things happened at school today. One thing was really good. And the other thing was very, very bad and tragical. ☹

THINGS THAT HAPPENED AT SCHOOL TODAY

The really GOOD thing

1 Ms Weiss told our class that we will be having a class Christmas disco on Friday! Yay! There's going to be:

XMAS PARTY Disco DANCING

XMAS PARTY FOOD

HO HO DRESS-UP COSTUMES (ME)

XMAS Games

And we're also having a Kris Kringle.* I picked Amethyst's name out of the hat. And I already know exACTly what excellent present I'm going to get for her.

fancy
Purple
LACES

I wonder what present I'll get?

* A Kris Kringle is when you pick a name out of a hat and then you have to buy a present for that person. And then you get one from someone who picked YOUR name out of a hat. It is all VERY mysterious and fun.

KRIS KRINGLE

(NAME)

inside
OF
HAT

The very, very bad and tragical thing

2 Peach Parker, who is the meanerest, most annoyingest person in the entire ~~world~~ ~~galaxy~~ universe (and also the UN-modest person I was talking about yesterday), handed out envelopes after school to all the girls in our class.

Peach Parker

Meanerest Girl IN THE Universe

All the girls except for TWO, that is.

And guess who THEY were???

Prinny and Jade each got an envelope, of course. They're Peach's BFFs. And her second-best friends, Esther and Fabrizia and Jaime and Amira, got them too. But so did Chloe and Georgia and Poppy. Which is just WEIRD. They're Zoe's and MY friends more than Peach's.

Even Cordelia got one. Peach doesn't even LIKE Cordelia. And Cordelia definitely, positively, absoLUTEly doesn't like Peach, especially after what she did to Mr Wombat at school camp.

FLAG POLE

MR WOMBAT

Cordelia showed Zoe and me her envelope on our way home. It was pale pink with little red hearts down the side, and her name was written on the front in fancy writing.

And inside it was an invitation to a Christmas party Peach is having next week at her house.

Dear _Cordelia_

You are invited to the Christmas garden party event of the year.

WHO BY: Peach Parker ♥

WHEN: Saturday 22 December at 2pm

WHERE: The Gables, 22 Calico Drive

WHAT: Delicious food and exclusive party activities

DRESS: Christmas Chic

RSVP: by Monday 17 December
⭐ on 5555 6848 ⭐

Bleuchhh. Who wants to
go to Princess Peach's silly
garden party anyway?
And why does she want
her guests to dress up
as chickens???

CHRISTMAS
Chic

Cordelia said she's not going, because she
has violin lessons on Saturday afternoons.
But even if she didn't, she told us NO
WAY would she go.

I bet everyone else
will though. ☹

Tuesday afternoon, after school

Everyone was talking about Peach's party at school today.

Chloe (shiny-eyed): Peach's party is going to be AMAZING. There's going to be a pony and pony rides.

PONY Rides

Georgia (even more shiny-eyed): And cookie-decorating tables and card-making stations.

cookie decorating

Poppy (shiny-eyed to the power of 10): And yummy food like individual mini-pizzas shaped like Christmas trees.

Mini Pizzas

Georgia: And Christmas-cake pops.

christmas-CAKE pops

Chloe: And don't forget about the punch.

Zoe (puzzled): Punch?

PUNCH

Chloe: It's a type of drink served in a big glass bowl with exotic fruits and clinking ice blocks and little umbrellas floating on the top. Peach showed me a picture from a magazine and it looked EXCELLENT.

Poppy: It is going to be the best party ever. I can't wait. Can you, Ella?

Me: Erm . . . Oooo, sorry, have to go. Ms Weiss is waving at me from the other side of the yard. She probably wants me to do something REALLY important for her.

which was just a big porky pie.* Ms Weiss
wasn't even in the yard. I just made that
up so I didn't have to say I hadn't been
invited.

* A porky pie is a big fat lie.

It's so not fair, Diary. Chloe and
Georgia and Poppy are supposed to
be MY friends, not Princess Peach's.
She probably won't even talk to
them at the party.

Chloe

GEORGIA

POPPY

At least I don't have to dress up like a chicken. Bleuchhh.

B-Gerk!

Bye,
Ella

Tuesday night, in bed

Dearest Diary,

Mum and Dad went to a Christmas party at Dad's work tonight. So Nanna Kate came round to cook dinner for Olivia and Max and me.

We had shepherd's pie* and
banana splits. (My favourite.)

* Shepherd's pie isn't
~~acksh~~ actually made out
of shepherds, in case you
were wondering. That would
be weird. It is made out of
meaty bits and mashed
potato and some other stuff.

After dinner, Nanna Kate helped us to make
an Advent calendar** out of cardboard.
We're going to put it up in the kitchen. (There
are only **15 days** till Christmas though,
so we got to eat the spare chocolates. YUM!)

Cardboard
Chocolates GO HERE
Tiny Houses
ADVENT CALENDAR

** An Advent calendar is a special calendar that counts down the days in December, which is the month that Christmas lives in. And there's a tiny house for each day and you can put little surprises or chocolates inside. And every day you open a door, so you know how many days there are left until Christmas.

Love,
Ella

Tuesday night, about ten minutes later

I wonder if Peach was planning to make invitations for Zoe and me all along but she ran out of pink envelopes and matching writing paper and is waiting until she can get more from the invitation shop?

Tuesday night, about five minutes after that

Or maybe she DID make invitations for us but they accidentally got lost or fell out of her bag on her way to school?

Yes. That must be it.

LOST invitations

ELLA

ZOE

Tuesday night, about five minutes after that

My **Operation Merry Christmas** is going to be way betterer and more fun than Peach's BORING party anyway.

I'm going to look up more snow recipes in the library at school tomorrow.

Wish me luck!

Ella xx

snow
Recipe

Wednesday night, after dinner

OMC STAGE TWO: Making SNOW (PART 2)

I found a recipe for homemade snow in this really excellent book from the library. I tried it out when I got home from school.

All I needed was:

BI CARB
SODA

Packet of
bicarb
SODA

Glass
BOWL

tubes of
Glitter

coconut
DREAM
H A I R
Conditioner

~~Forth~~ Fortunately there was a big packet of bicarb soda in the kitchen cupboard.

I poured the bicarb soda and the hair conditioner into the bowl. Then I sprinkled a whole tube of sparkly glitter on top and squisherised everything with my hands until it turned into snow.

It was aMAZing! And EXcellent!

But very, very small. ☹

How are you supposed to
go tobogganing or make
snow angels or build snow
forts if you only have one
teeny, tiny ball of snow?

Thursday, after school

Dear Diary,

Georgia said today that there is going to be a photo booth at Peach's party. And you can have your make-up and hair done by a ~~profesh~~ professional make-up lady and get dressed up in a fancy red velvet Christmas frock. With angel wings. And a ~~hello~~ halo.

Halo

Angel Wings

Sweetheart Neckline

Flared Skirt

Fancy RED Velvet

(FAKE) WHITE FUR

But I STILL don't have an invitation. ☹

And neither does Zoe. ☹☹

Thursday, five minutes later

I hope everyone gets Occhilupo's Disease*
so they can't go.

* Occhilupo's Disease is
this disease I made up once
when I didn't want to go to

Occhilupo's
Disease

school. You get a hurterous itchy red rash all over your tummy and it is HIGHLY ~~CONTAJUS~~ CONTAGIOUS. (Which means it is easy to catch it from people who already have it.)

I have to go, Diary, someone is ringing the doorbell! Maybe it is Peach delivering our invitations!!!

Thursday, after dinner

The Bad News
It wasn't.

The Good News

It was Nanna Kate.

Nanna KATE

She'd come to take me late-night shopping to buy my Kris Kringle present for Amethyst, for our class disco tomorrow.

And when we got home, we made reindeer cupcakes to take as well. They started out as plain old cupcakes that looked like this.

(PLAIN CUPCAKES)

Then we iced them with chocolate icing and stuck lollies and pretzels on them to make their little faces. Don't they look sweet?

← REINDEER **CUPCAKES**

Yours 4 EVER,
Ella xx

Friday night, in bed

Dear Diary,

We had our class disco today. It was
fantabulously fabulous!

After recess, we all got dressed up in our BEST outfits. Here's what I wore. I spent all last night putting it together.

Tiara

my favourite ♥ glittery T-Shirt

Feather BOA

RIDING BOOTS (with XMAS glitter ★ Stars taped to the FRONT)

BEST ♥ Ballet Tutu

We played lots of fun Christmas games like:

Christmas LiMBO

NOSE

Pin the NOSE on the REINDEER

?? Guess what's inside the CHRISTMAS STOCKING

Then our excellent teacher Ms Weiss put on some VERY LOUD CHRISTMAS MUSIC so we could all dance. Even the boys danced!!!

Bleuchhh. Boys should just be BANNED from dancing.

Then we ate all the Christmas party food. Everyone said my reindeer cupcakes were the BEST.

MY CUPCAKES

And Ms Weiss handed out the presents for the Kris Kringle.

This is what I got.

I bet I know who they came from.

(ZOE)

Today was EXcellently excellent.

It was exACTly the kind of fun day I want to have at our house this Christmas.

I have to find out a good way to make snow. I just HAVE to!

Good night, Diary.
Love,
Ella

Saturday morning, before breakfast

Dear Diary,

I woke up really early so I could be the firsterest one to get the chocolate out of the next little door on our Advent calendar.

But the little door was all munched off!

And there was something squisherous and slimy inside!

And my finger touched it!

And guess what it was?

E x

Saturday, after breakfast

I am in desperating despair, Diary!

Everything is hopelessly hopeless.

WHY EVERYTHING is
HOPELESSLY Hopeless

1 So far, **OMC** is NOT excellent or
amazing or fantabulously fabulous.
I only have a few decorations and I can't
make enough snow.

2 There are squisherous snails in the
Advent calendar, eating all our chocolates.

3 Peach is never, ever, EVER in a million
pazillion years going to invite Zoe and
me to her party.

There is only one thing to do.

Have an EPM✻ with Zoe. I'm
going to call her RIGHT NOW.

✻ EPM = Emergency Phone Meeting.

Saturday morning, about an hour later

Dearest Diary,

Zoe and I had our EPM.

And guess what?

We are going to . . .

wait for it . . .

Are you ready?

(Hehehe.)

We are going to SNEAK IN to Peach's
Christmas garden party! (Hehehe.)

There is only one small snag with our plan.
Peach's house has a giganterous, EXtremely
high brick wall all around it. So giganterous
and so high it is imPOSSible to the power
of 10 gatrillion to climb over it. So we
thought up some sneaky ways to get inside.

SNEAKY WAYS TO SNEAK INTO PEACH'S PARTY, AND CHANCE OF THEM WORKING

Sneaky way	Chance	Reason why/ why not
① Hire a helicopter and lower ourselves down into Peach's garden with ropes.	0%	We don't have enough money and anyway, I am exTREMEly scared of heights. And helicopters.

ZOE ME

2 Throw ninja grappling hooks onto the wall and climb over, ninja-style, and drop (stealthily) into the garden.

0%

Zoe and I are both exTREMEly good at ninja moves. But we don't have any ninja grappling hooks.

3 Set up a ~~tramper teen~~ trampoline on our side of the wall and do a giganterous bounce into Peach's garden.

0%

We don't have a trampoline. And even if we did, we might get tangled in the safety netting when we did our big jump off it.

4 Dig a deeperous tunnel under the wall.

0%

Our party outfits would get dirty and they would know it was us straightaway. Plus we might get lost and end up in China.

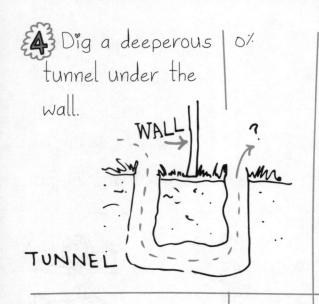

WALL →

?

TUNNEL

5 Pretend to be clowns from a clown hire place, who are coming to the party to do a funny clown show for the party guests.

100%

Zoe's Aunty Ornella works in a fancy dress shop, so we can easily get some clown outfits and make-up. Plus everyone is always telling us we are very funny (hehe).

YESSSS! This last one is PERFECT for us! We can be TOP-SECRET undercover clown agents! Sneaking into Precious Peach's Perfect Party will be EASY-PEASY.

Saturday afternoon

Dearest Diary,

Working out what to do about one of the hopelessly hopeless things made me feel MUCH betterer. So I decided to get straight back to work on **OMC** to make our Christmas excellent and fabulous again!

OMC STAGE TWO: Making SNOW (PART 3)

While Mum was out shopping, Dad helped me to find a video on the computer about how to make snow.

It was aMAZing. The girl in the video put some special crystally things in a bowl and poured a glass of water on the top of them and **HEY ZINGO!**

The crystals started getting bigger

and bigger

and bigger

until they were expanding and erupting and exploding everywhere, just like one of the volcanoes in the Natural Disasters of the world project we did at school last term. The mixture went up the sides of the bowl and over the top and spread out all over the table and onto the floor.

And guess what?

It looked just like snow!
Frosty, snow-flaky snow.

And there was heaps of it!

I was SO EXCITERATED!

But then on the next
part of the video I
found out where the
girl got the special
crystals from.

Nappies.

Those things that babies wear to soak up all their stinky baby pee. Eww.

Eww.

AND she had to tear up about a gatrillion nappies to get enough crystals to make the snow.

a Gatrillion NAPPIES

No way am I ever going to be able to buy that many nappies, even if I saved up all my birthday and Christmas and pocket money for the next pazillion years.

Saturday afternoon, about fifteen minutes later

I was just about to ask Dad if we could all move to an exTREMEly cold place, like Iceland or the North Pole, where there are polar bears and penguins and it snows ALL YEAR ROUND. Which means you don't have to worry about making it yourself. But then Dad came out carrying the big box of Christmas decorations from the top cupboard.

ICELAND   North Pole

ME

Penguin

Polar Bear

While we were hanging the decorations, Max and Olivia reminded me we hadn't written our Christmas wish lists yet! How will Santa know what presents to bring us if we don't write our lists!!!???

So I got out my best glitter pens and put on some VERY LOUD Christmas music like Ms Weiss played for our class disco and we all sat down at the kitchen table and wrote our lists. (I helped Max write his.)

To Santa
c/o The North Pole

Dear **Santa.**
Please can you bring me:

A stylish HandBAG like

Ms Weiss's

A **Giganterous** BOX of GEL AND Glitter Pens

A {NEW} **PET** (hopefully a **SLOTH** because they are extremely ~~CUTE~~ and **ADORABLE**)

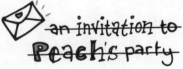

~~an invitation to Peach's party~~

SLOTH

Love ♥ ♥
ELLA xoxo

To Santa ~~Claws~~ Claus
The North Pole

Dear Santa. I would like:

- a tiara like Ella's

- a book about ~~norty~~ naughty princesses

- a whoopee cushion to trick Dad

- a new bike (a black one, with red flames)

Thanks! Olivia

To Santa Claus'
THE NORTH POLE

Dear **Santa**.

I have been a very **GOOD** and helpful **BOY** all year.

Please can I have:

• a **PiRate SHiP**

• Snail food FoR my **PET** Snail collection

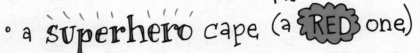

• a tramper leen

• a **superhero** cape (a **RED** one)

Love
Max

Have to go now, Diary. Mum is back from shopping and she wants me to set the table for dinner. She is making spaghetti with cheesy meatballs.

Yours 4 EVER,
Ella xx

Sunday, after lunch

Dear Diary,

Zoe just rang to say
she has something
amazing to tell me
and is coming over
IMMEDIATELY for an emergency

I wonder what the something is?

I CAN'T WAIT TO FIND OUT!!

Sunday night, in bed

Dearest, darlingest Diary,

You will never EVER believe
what happened this afternoon
so I will just tell you.

I was just tidying away all of the
ASSORTED ESSENTIAL STUFF* that lives on
my bed so we would have a clear space to
sit for our emergency Emergency Meeting
when Zoe bounced into my room like a
bouncy bouncing ball and said, 'Guess what?'

BOUNCE bounce

* ASSORTED ESSENTIAL STUFF:

MATCHING **CUSHIONS**

♥ SHEEPIE ♥

spare packet OF **GLITTER PENS** in case the other ones run out

Pyjama **CASE**

BOOKS about EXOTIC **ANIMALS**

Zoe's eyes were super shiny, the way they go when she is really exciterated about something. SO exciterated I knew straightaway that if she didn't tell me what it was IMMEDIATELY, she would burst like

Shiny EYES

ZOE

a birthday balloon when your dad ~~acksa~~ accidentally blows it up too far.

So instead of having three long and complicated guesses like I usually do, I just said, 'WHAT?'

Zoe looked a bit shocked. Then she told me her big brother, Will, was at a Christmas party yesterday and they had snow!

And then she showed me a photo of Will and his friends frolicking around in it.

❄ Will and his friends

Except it wasn't real snow. It was foam!
Foamerous bubbly foam, like when you
accidentally put too
much bubble bath
in the bath and
leave the hot water
tap running and the
foamy bubbles go
EVERYWHERE!

The snow-foam came out of a special
complicated-looking machine. I was just about
to say we would never have enough money in
a fabrillion years to buy one of those when
Zoe whispered a secret in my ear.

A **TOP-SECRET** secret that is SO secret I am not going to write it down in case someone finds you and reads it and tells Mum before Christmas Day!

And that would **RUIN EVERYTHING!**

So I'm just going to keep it in the topperest part of my brain for now.

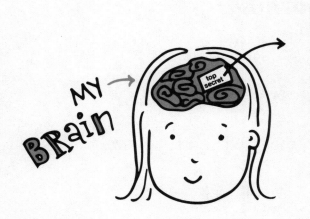

MY BRAIN

FOR OMC STAGE TWO

After Zoe went home, I asked Dad if he can help me to make the TOP-SECRET secret thing. And he said YES!

The first thing we'll need is a big plastic barrel.

Good night, Diary.
Ella xx

Monday morning

Dear Diary,

I just had the most aMAZing dream!

The MOST AMAZING DREAM

Dad and Olivia and Max and Nanna Kate and I were all sitting around a picnic table outside our caravan, right next to the swimming pool. And we were drinking Christmassy cold drinks and eating Christmas food and reading out the jokes from our Christmas crackers.

Except our caravan wasn't in Moonlight Bay. It was in our own backyard! I could see our big flowering gum tree which is always full of squawky parrots, and Dad's tomato plants in the vegie patch.

And then a big sleigh full of exciting and expensive-looking presents arrived, pulled by Dasher and Crasher and Rude-off and Bob.

Dasher   Crasher   RUDE-OFF   BOB

And guess who was sitting smack-bang right in the middle of the sleigh?

HINT: It rhymes with

(rhymes)

And she said, 'Thank you, Ella sweetheart darling. This has been the Best Christmas Ever.'

And you'll never guess what happened next!

It SNOWED!!!

I can't wait to talk to Zoe about what my dream means, so I have to stop writing now, Diary, and get ready for school. There's only **2 days** of school left for the whole year!

Love,
E

Monday, after school

Zoe and I spent ALL lunchtime talking about my exciterating dream. And it made me realise something REALLY IMPORTERANT:

We don't have to be in Moonlight Bay to have a good Christmas. The whole family can have an excellent time right here in our own backyard!

Now I know what I have to do:

✳ **OMC** 〈 **STAGE THREE** 〉 ∘ ✳

Set up our BACKYARD to Look Like 〈MOONLIGHT GARDENS CARAVAN PARK ✳

It is going to be fanTABulously FABulous.

✳ Ask Dad for help.

(Again. ☺)

I can't wait to get started! I've worked out everything we'll need:

Picnic table AND CHAIRS

SLeeping BAGS for a nice relaxing lie-down after christmas LUNCH.

Paddling POOL for swimming

Soft Drink

ICE

ESKY

icy-cold COLD DRINKS

TENT

Tent (an ~~acksh~~ actual, **real** caravan wouldn't fit in our backyard so this will have to do)

And then we'll make our own ~~homemade~~
~~foam machine so we can make snow~~

TOP
SECRET

OMC
TOP-SECRET
Secret
thing under
HERE

Monday night, in bed

Dear Diary-doo,

Tomorrow is the last day of school! I made Ms Weiss a present. Isn't it beautiful?

WORLD'S
MOST
excellentest
TEACHER

She is going to LOVE it for sure! ☺☺☺

CYA.
Love,
Ella

Tuesday, after school

Ms Weiss DID love my special present!

Ms Weiss

MY
SPECIAL
PRESENT

Here are the other presents she got from our class:

1 Bottle of **PERFUME**

3 COFFEE **MUGS**

5 **CHRISTMAS CANDLES**

7 **Bars** OF **SMELLY Soap**

9 **Boxes** OF **CHOCOLATES**

and a par-trrrriiiidge in a pear tree! ♫ ♩ ♪
(Only joking! ☺)

Then we all called out soppy things to each other like:

Have good HOLiDAYS!

See YOU at the POOL!

Have a GOOD christmas!

(Except ZOE and I didn't say this one because **no-one's** expecting to see **US** there - hehe.)

See you on **Saturday** at the **PARTY!**

And then that was it.

NO MORE SCHOOL FOR SIX WHOLE WEEKS!

YAAAAAAAAAAAAAAYYYYYYY!

See you later, Diary.

Wednesday night, in bed

Dearest Diary,

Today Dad and I worked on getting everything ready for **OMC STAGE THREE**.

First of all, we organised the rest of the things we need for the TOP-SECRET OMC secret:

A long HOSE connected to a tap

A large Bottle of BUBBLE BATH LIQUID

Rope

Wet and DRY Vacuum cleaner

A beach TOWEL

A ROLL of duct tape

Then I made some homemade Christmas crackers, and wrote special locater-ising clues to put inside, instead of jokes. I'm going to hide them around the house and get Mum to search for them. And each clue will help her to find where the next one is hidden!

CHRISTMAS CRACKERS
(HOME MADE)

Locater-ising CLUES inside

Down and up, hup hup hup
You climb these every day!

This is the place you have to go
When you want to wash your toe

And the very last clue will lead her outside into the garden for the special Christmas surprise!

It is SO EXCITERATING! Only **6 days** till Christmas!

Good night, Diary.

E xx

Thursday night

Zoe came around today to go over our undercover plan for how we are going to sneak into Peach's party on Saturday. We spent all afternoon practising clown routines, just in case anyone asks us to do something funny and clownerous once we're inside the gates.

Zoe's mum is going to take us to her Aunty Ornella's fancy dress shop tomorrow so we can choose our clown outfits.

Everything is set!
CYA L8R, Diary!
Ella

Friday, after dinner

Dearest Diary,

Zoe and I found the most stylishly stylish clown costumes at her aunty's fancy dress shop this morning. No-one will EVER be able to tell that it's us!

And while I was there, I saw all these really sweet little costumes for dogs, and I thought why don't I get a REINDEER outfit for Bob? It would be perfect for OMC!

But the only thing they had in his size was a goat. Which is a bit like a reindeer. So we got that one.

MAAAAH

BOB
(the goat!)

And then guess who we saw at the shopping centre?

You got it.

Peach and her best
buddies, Prinny and Jade.
They were carrying big
shopping bags full of
goodies for her garden party
tomorrow.

Peach gave me a BIG SNEERY SMIRK.

So I gave her a BIG SNEERY SMIRK right
back.

Peach   ← Sneery   Me
         SMIRK →

Hehe. She doesn't know what WE know.

I can't wait to sneak into her party tomorrow. ☺

Yours 4 ever,
Ella (the clown)

Saturday night, in bed

Dearest Diary,

Today was aMAZing! And exCELLent!
And a little bit SCARY!

We arrived at Peach's house at exactly 1.55 pm, dressed in our (stylish) undercover clown outfits. We hid behind the bus shelter across the street so we could ~~covurtly~~ ~~cavertly~~ secretly watch people as they arrived.

ZOE

ME

BUS

SHELTER

We saw Prinny and Jade go in, wearing matchy-matchy outfits. And then Esther and Fabrizia went in, and Jaime and Amira, and all the bun-head girls from gymnastics, and Poppy and Georgia and Chloe. (No-one was dressed like a chicken.)

After about fifteen minutes of waiting, I sent Zoe a series of complicated hand signals to see if she thought it was time to get started with our plan.

Zoe sent me a series of complicated hand
signals back to say, 'Yes.'

So we strolled (clownishly) over to a set of
big gates and knocked on them three times.
A man wearing a security badge opened them.

Here's what happened
next:

Security Man (sternly):
what do you two want?

Zoe (clownishly): Umm . . .
We're the clowns that Peach's
mum . . . I mean, Mrs Parker
hired to do the clown show.

(ZOE)

Security Man (looking at a list):
There's no clown show on the program.
Me (using all my powers of persuasion I
normally use on Mum when I want something
really, really badly, like a new packet of gel
pens, or pony-riding lessons): Oh, ple-e-e-ase
let us in, kind sir. Peach's mum . . . I mean,
Mrs Parker obviously forgot to put our
names on the list.
Security Man (suspiciously): What are your
names?
Zoe: Binky . . . and . . . umm . . . Stinky.

Me (inside my head): Binky and Stinky??!?
Thanks, Zoe (not).
Me (out loud): That's right. Binky and Stinky.
And our show starts in ten minutes.

And then guess what happened?

The security man
let us into Peach's
garden party! It
looked aMAZing! And
fanTABulously fabulous!

There were card-making stations and a pony
for riding and individual mini-pizzas shaped
like Christmas trees and a photo booth and
red velvet dresses, just like Georgia and
Poppy and Chloe said there'd be.

And sitting on a kind
of throne in the
middle of the garden
was Princess Peach,
surrounded by presents.

PEACH

We were just sneaking stealthily over to
the food table to get some Christmas-tree
mini-pizzas when something horrendously
horrible happened.

I tripped over my floppy clown shoes and landed—**SPLAT**—facedown in the bowl of punch. Clinking ice cubes and exotic fruits and little umbrellas went everywhere!

And then Peach's little sister Petunia said, 'Oooooo, look, Mummy! Funny clowns! Make them do it again!'

And then everyone started laughing and clapping, like they thought we were REAL clowns, doing a REAL show!

So we did one, just like we'd practised. Zoe walked around on her hands and did a backflip. And I did a funny kind of clown dance, and squirted Prinny and Jade with my trick flower.

And then Zoe and I pretended to crash into each other.

And everyone laughed again.

We were just leaning over to do our bows when something even MORE horrendously horrible happened.

My clown wig fell off.

NOOOOOOOOOoo...!!

And then Prinny called out,
'That's not a REAL clown. That's Ella!'

And Jade yelled, 'And I bet
that other one's Zoe!'

And Peach screeched, 'How
DARE they be at MY party.'

So we raced out of the big
gates before the security
man could stop us.

And guess what?

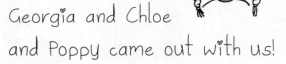

Georgia and Chloe
and Poppy came out with us!

They said Peach's party was BORING! Peach
wouldn't let anyone ride the pony except
for her. And Prinny and Jade and their other
friends hogged the photo booth and the
card-making stuff the WHOLE TIME.
Poppy said the only fun part was when Zoe
and I turned up!

So then Georgia's mum drove us all to the
Ice-cream Shoppe for triple-decker ice-
creams. With nuts and caramel sauce.

And now I am EXHAUSTERATED.
But happy too. ☺

Good night, Diary.
Sweet dreams.
Ella x

Sunday morning, before lunch

Only TWO more sleeps to go until
Christmas! I can't wait to see what
everyone thinks of all my **OMC** surprises
(especially Mum)!!!

Here's a poem I wrote, just for you!

I
love
the smells
and the sounds
and the tastes of
my favourite season
******CHRISTMAS!******
Bells are ringing and people
are singing and cakes are baking
and families are making lists for gifts
and cards and presents for CHRISTMAS!
There are reindeers on roofs—with shiny red
noses—the vases are filled with lilies and roses,
I've hung up my stocking, left Santa a treat, now I'm

waiting
waiting
waiting
waiting
waiting
waiting
waiting

for him to arrive in our street!
It's joyful and jolly and full of
good cheer. How I wish it
was ***CHRISTMAS***
each day of the year!

Monday morning, early

Good morning, Diary.

Just wanted to wish you a very merry Christmas Eve.

Have to go now. There is HEAPS to do to get ready for tomorrow!

Tuesday night, late, in bed

Dearest, darlingest Diary,

There is just so much to tell you!

After breakfast, Nanna Kate took Mum over to Zoe's place to have Christmas morning tea with Zoe's mum, so Dad and Olivia and Max and I could get everything ready.

When they were gone, Max and Olivia hid the Christmas Cracker Clues around the house while I set up our special 'caravan park' in the garden.

Then Dad and I put together our **TOP-SECRET** Secret **OMC** Machine.

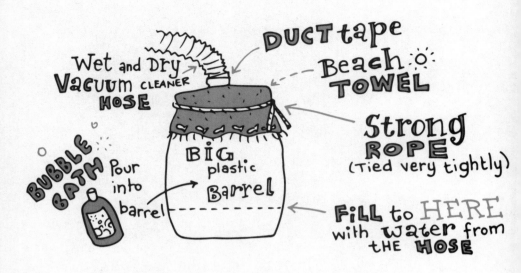

Wet and Dry **VACUUM** CLEANER **HOSE**

DUCT tape

Beach ☼ **TOWEL**

Strong ROPE (Tied very tightly)

BUBBLE BATH Pour into barrel

BIG plastic **Barrel**

FILL to HERE with **water** from **THE HOSE**

Dad put some water and bubble bath inside and then hid it behind the flowering gum tree.

DAD

water

bubble bath

TOP-SECRET Secret

And guess what? Everything worked out
fantabulously fabulously!

Mum and Nanna Kate came home and saw
the first Christmas Cracker Clue taped to
the front door. And
then we all helped
Mum to find the
other clues hidden
around the house.

First CLUE

I thought the last one was REALLY tricky.

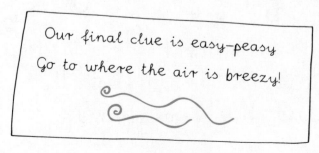

Our final clue is easy-peasy
Go to where the air is breezy!

But Mum worked it out straightaway! She came out into the garden, just like she was supposed to, and sat down in her special deckchair.

MUM

And then . . .

Tadaaaaaa!

Dad started up the vacuum cleaner. And lovely, white, sparkly, flufferous snow-foam came

cascading

out of the top of our foam-making machine and built up and up and up until the WHOLE GARDEN was covered in it.

And we frolicked around and made
snow people and had snow fights with
snow-foam-balls and built snow forts to
hide in, just like I planned.

Then we had a giganterous picnic and
opened all our presents and played garden
cricket and totem tennis all afternoon.

And guess what Mum said to me at the end
of the day?

Good night, Diary.
MERRY CHRISTMAS!
YOURS 4 EVER,
Ella
xOx

PS (five minutes later)

I forgot to tell you what Santa brought me for Christmas!

SLOTH onesie

Stylish Hand BAG

CHUNKY Beads

GeL AND Glitter Pehs

Stylish BELT

a BOX of CHOCOLATES

Books ON Fashion

ELLA Diaries

Read more of Ella's brilliant diary in

Double Dare You

Ballet Backflip

I ♥ Pets

Dreams come true

Christmas CHAOS

Pony School Showdown

FRIENDS NOT FOREVER

WORST CAMP EVER

and look out for more coming soon!